# Stephanie's Ponytail

# Stephanie's Ponytail

STORY by
ROBERT MUNSCH

ART by
MICHAEL MARTCHENKO

annick press
toronto • berkeley

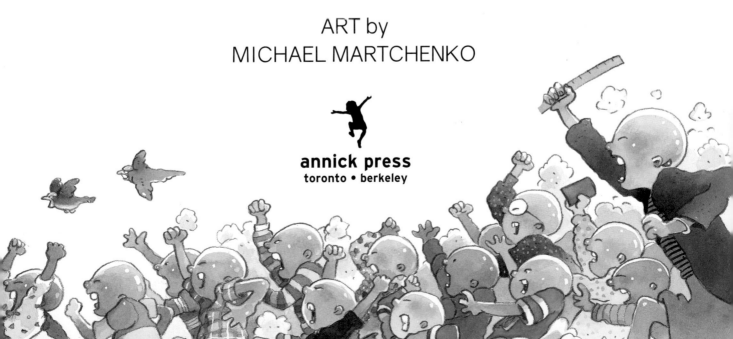

We acknowledge the support of the Canada Council for the Arts and the Ontario Arts Council, and the participation of the Government of Canada/la participation du gouvernement du Canada for our publishing activities.

ONTARIO ARTS COUNCIL
CONSEIL DES ARTS DE L'ONTARIO
an Ontario government agency
un organisme du gouvernement de l'Ontario

Library and Archives Canada Cataloguing in Publication

Munsch, Robert N., 1945-, author
    Stephanie's ponytail / Robert Munsch ; illustrated by Michael Martchenko. -- Classic Munsch edition.

Originally published in 1996.
ISBN 978-1-77321-036-0 (hardcover).--ISBN 978-1-77321-035-3 (softcover)

    I. Martchenko, Michael, illustrator  II. Title.

PS8576.U575S74 2018          jC813'.54          C2017-905735-9

Published in the U.S.A. by Annick Press (U.S.) Ltd.
Distributed in Canada by University of Toronto Press.
Distributed in the U.S.A. by Publishers Group West.

Printed in China

www.annickpress.com
www.robertmunsch.com

Also available in e-book format. Please visit www.annickpress.com/ebooks.html for more details.

To Stephanie Caswell,
Durham, Ontario

One day Stephanie went to her mom and said, "None of the kids in my class has a ponytail. I want a nice ponytail coming right out the back."

So Stephanie's mom gave her a nice ponytail coming right out the back.

When Stephanie went to school, the other kids looked at her and said, "Ugly, Ugly, **VERY UGLY**."

Stephanie said, "It's *my ponytail* and **I LIKE IT**."

The next morning, when Stephanie went to school, all the other girls had ponytails coming out the back.

Stephanie looked at them and said, "You are all a bunch of copycats. You just do whatever I do. You don't have a brain in your heads."

The next morning the mom said, "Stephanie, would you like a ponytail coming out the back?"

Stephanie said, "**NO**."

"Then that's that," said her mom. "That's the only place you can do ponytails."

"No, it's not," said Stephanie. "I want one coming out the side, just above my ear."

"Very strange," said the mom. "Are you sure that is what you want?"

"Yes," said Stephanie.

So her mom gave Stephanie a nice ponytail coming out right above her ear.

When she went to school, the other kids saw her and said, "Ugly, Ugly, **VERY UGLY**."

Stephanie said, "It's *my ponytail* and **I LIKE IT**."

The next morning, when Stephanie came to school, all the girls, and even some of the boys, had nice ponytails coming out just above their ears.

The next morning the mom said, "Stephanie, would you like a ponytail coming out the back?"

Stephanie said, "**NNNO**."

"Would you like one coming out the side?"

"**NNNO**."

"Then that's that," said her mom. "There is no other place you can do ponytails."

"Yes, there is," said Stephanie. "I want one coming out of the top of my head like a tree."

"That's very, very strange," said her mom. "Are you sure that is what you want?"

"Yes," said Stephanie.

So her mom gave Stephanie a nice
ponytail coming out of the top of her
head like a tree. When Stephanie went to
school, the other kids saw her and said,
"Ugly, Ugly, **VERY UGLY**."

Stephanie said, "It's *my ponytail*
and **I LIKE IT**."

The next day all of the girls and all of
the boys had ponytails coming out the top.
It looked like broccoli was growing out of
their heads.

The next morning the mom said, "Stephanie, would you like a ponytail coming out the back?"

Stephanie said, "**NNNO**."

"Would you like one coming out the side?"

"**NNNO**!"

"Would you like one coming out the top?"

"**NNNO**!"

"Then that is definitely that," said the mom. "There is no other place you can do ponytails."

"Yes, there is," said Stephanie. "I want one coming out the front and hanging down in front of my nose."

"But nobody will know if you are coming or going," her mom said. "Are you sure that is what you want?"

"Yes," said Stephanie. So her mom gave Stephanie a nice ponytail coming out the front.

On the way to school she bumped into four trees, three cars, two houses, and one Principal.

When she finally got to her class, the other kids saw her and said, "Ugly, ugly, **VERY UGLY**."

Stephanie said, "It's *my ponytail* and **I LIKE IT**."

The next day all of the girls and all of the boys, and even the teacher, had ponytails coming out the front and hanging down in front of their noses. None of them could see where they were going. They bumped into the desks and they bumped into each other. They bumped into the walls and, by mistake, three girls went into the boys' bathroom.

Stephanie yelled, "You are a bunch of brainless copycats. You just do whatever I do. When I come tomorrow, I am going to have . . . **SHAVED MY HEAD**!"

The first person to come the next day was the teacher. She had shaved her head and she was bald.

The next to come were the boys. They had shaved their heads and they were bald.

The next to come were the girls. They had shaved their heads and they were bald.

The last person to come was Stephanie, and she had . . .

a nice little ponytail coming right out the back.

Even More Classic Munsch:

The Dark
Mud Puddle
The Paper Bag Princess
The Boy in the Drawer
Jonathan Cleaned Up, Then He Heard a Sound
Millicent and the Wind
Mortimer
The Fire Station
Angela's Airplane
David's Father
Thomas' Snowsuit
50 Below Zero
I Have to Go!
Moira's Birthday
A Promise is a Promise
Pigs
Something Good
Show and Tell
Purple, Green and Yellow
Wait and See
Where is Gah-Ning?
From Far Away
Munschworks: The First Munsch Collection
Munschworks 2: The Second Munsch Treasury
Munschworks 3: The Third Munsch Treasury
Munschworks 4: The Fourth Munsch Treasury
The Munschworks Grand Treasury
Munsch Mini-Treasury One
Munsch Mini-Treasury Two
Munsch Mini-Treasury Three

For information on these titles please visit www.annickpress.com
Many Munsch titles are available in French and/or Spanish, as well as in
board book and e-book editions. Please contact your favorite supplier.